This book belongs to

⊛⊛⊛⊛⊛⊛⊛⊛⊛⊛⊛⊛⊛⊛⊛⊛⊛

For Namirembe and Nantale, and the dreams they laid beneath our feet.
Nansubuga

A tous les rêveurs du monde, grands et petits... To all dreamers, big and small.
Sandra

American edition published in 2017 by Lantana Publishing Ltd.
www.lantanapublishing.com

First published in the United Kingdom in 2017 by
Lantana Publishing Ltd., London.
info@lantanapublishing.com

Text © Nansubuga Nagadya Isdahl 2017
Illustration © Sandra van Doorn 2017

Distributed in the United States and Canada by Lerner Publishing Group, Inc.
241 First Avenue North
Minneapolis, MN 55401 USA

For reading levels and more information, look for this title at
www.lernerbooks.com.

Printed and bound in Hong Kong.
Cataloguing-in-Publication Data Available.

ISBN-13: 978-1-911373-09-4
eBook ISBN: 978-1-911373-20-9

SLEEP WELL
Siba & Saba

Nansubuga Nagadya Isdahl and Sandra van Doorn

LANTANA
PUBLISHING

Siba and Saba lost things.

Not a day slipped by when the sisters
hadn't lost something...

...somewhere.

They lost seven sweaters
in seven speeding buses.

They lost two pairs
of silver sandals

on the sandy beaches at Ssese Islands.

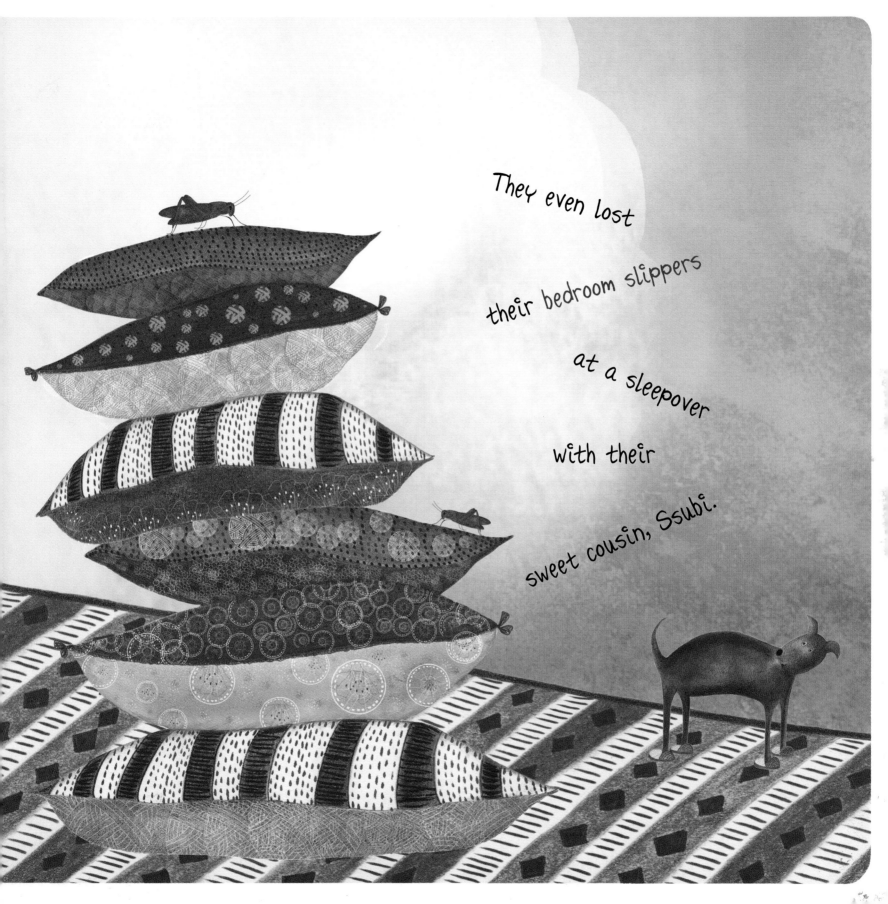

They even lost their bedroom slippers at a sleepover with their sweet cousin, Ssubi.

"Sula bulungi,
Siba and Saba,"

Papa would sing
before sending the
sisters to sleep.

"Sleep well,
Siba and Saba."

And in their sleep, between soft sheets
and dreams of sweets

they would find all the things they had lost.

Siba dreamed of her best satin sash

that she lost on safari with her ballet school class.

She dropped the sash in the savannah grass as she sat silently watching an impala pass.

Saba dreamed of her mama's shawl
that she lost on a stroll through
the sunlit Sipi Falls.

The soft wool shawl fell
out of her hand

as she watched a sunbird take off and land.

One night, Papa sang,
"Sula bulungi, Siba and Saba."

"Sleep well,
Siba and Saba."

And the sisters slept and they slept, but for once they did not dream of lost things.

Siba dreamed of a
silver shilling

settled in the side
pocket of a silk purse.

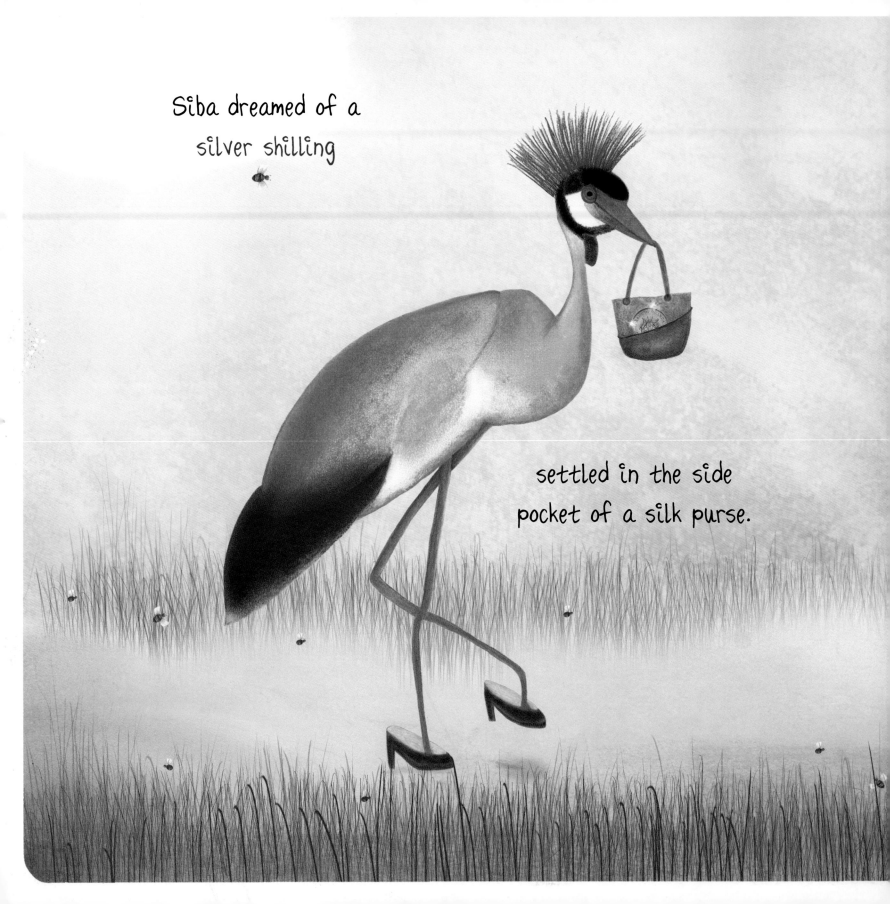

But she had never lost a silver shilling.

Saba dreamed of a stiffly
starched school uniform,
ready and waiting for a
smart student.

But she had never lost a stiffly
starched school uniform.

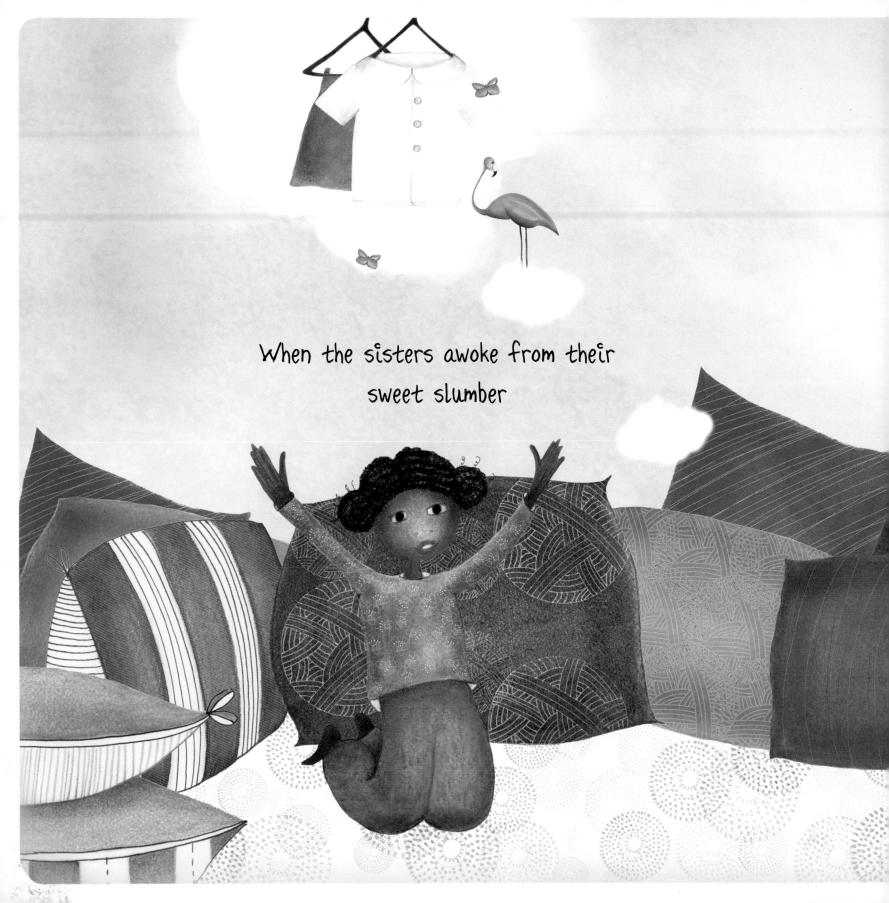

When the sisters awoke from their
sweet slumber

they shared with each other
the stories of the things they
had seen in their sleep.

"A silver shilling,"
said Siba.

"A school uniform,"
said Saba.

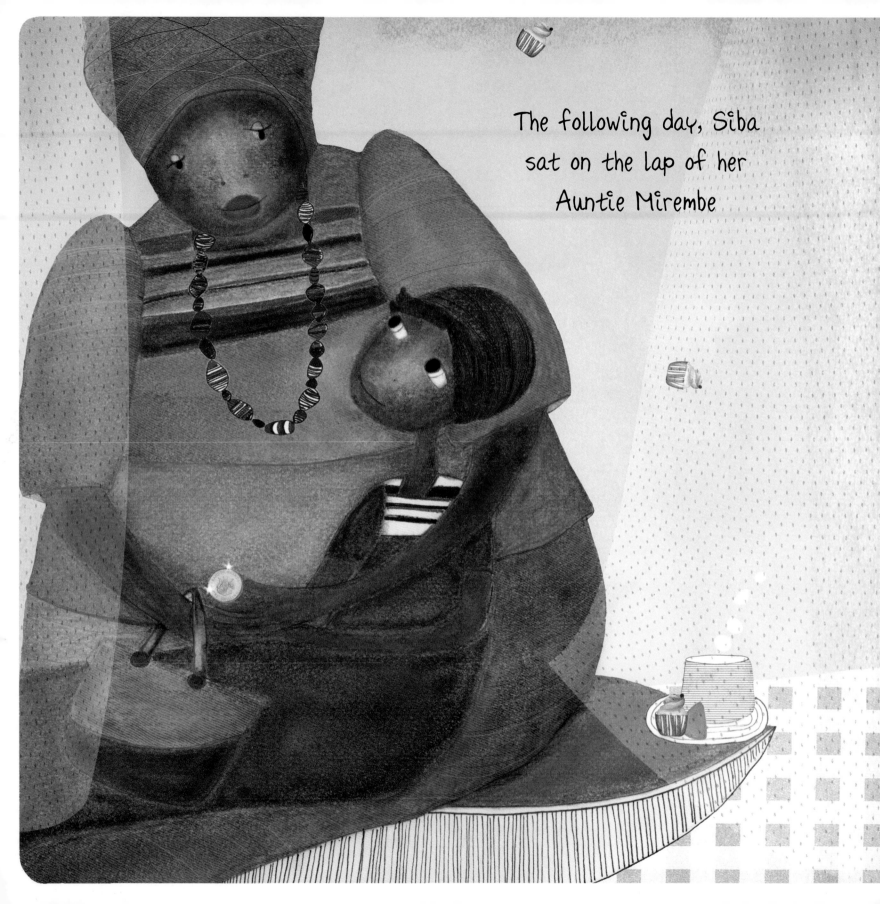

The following day, Siba
sat on the lap of her
Auntie Mirembe

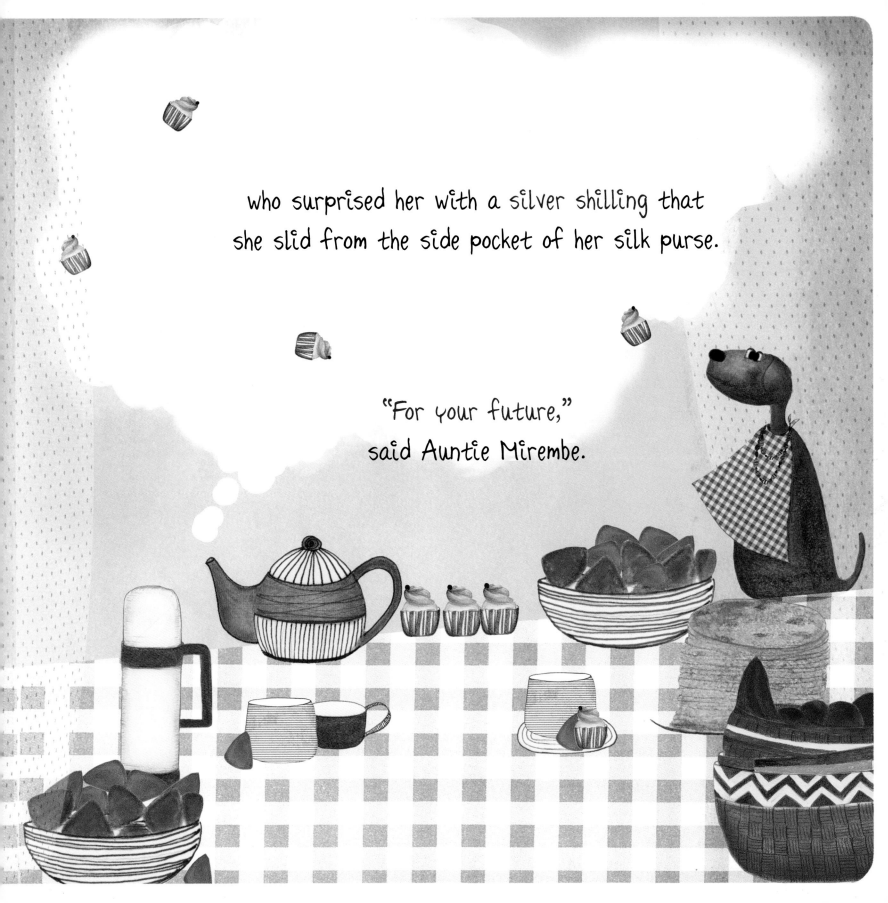

who surprised her with a silver shilling that
she slid from the side pocket of her silk purse.

"For your future,"
said Auntie Mirembe.

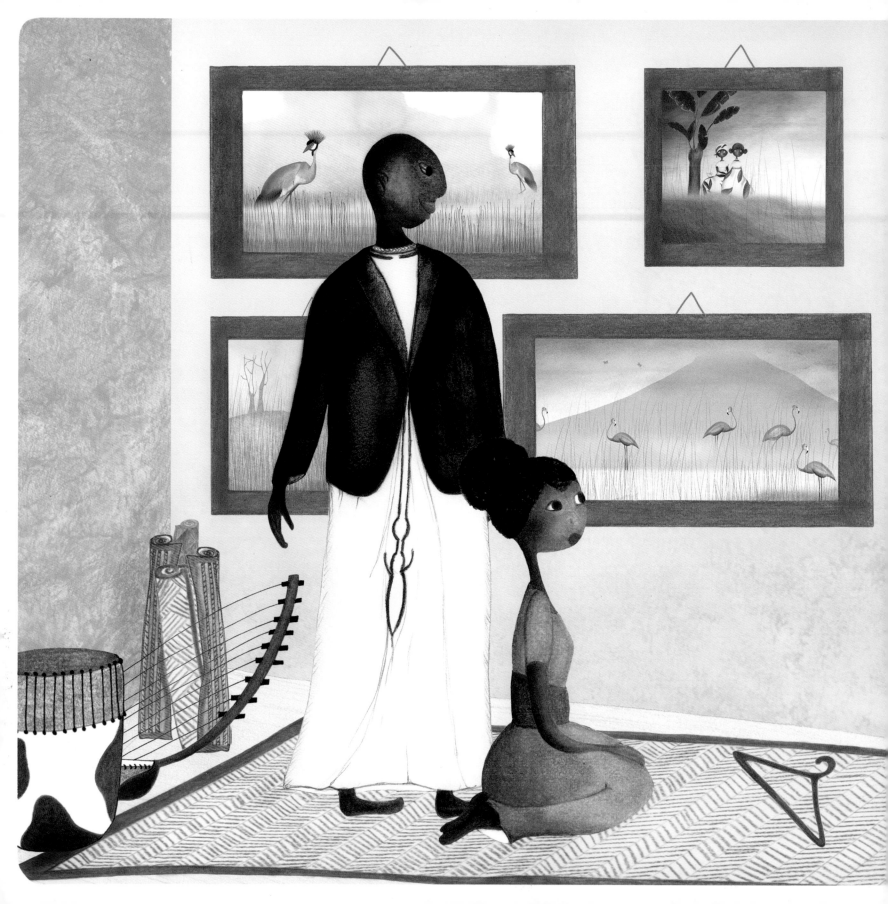

Later that evening, Papa came home with a new, stiffly starched school uniform for Saba, who was starting school soon.

"For your future," said Papa.

The sisters looked at each other and smiled.

And from that day on, Siba and Saba never again dreamed of the things they had lost.

They only dreamed about the special things they would someday see.

If you enjoyed this book,
why not try other picture books by

Lantana Publishing is an independent
publishing house producing award-winning
children's books by authors and illustrators
from around the world.

*Because all children
deserve to see themselves
in the books they read.*